LOCK-IN

JONATHAN MARY-TODD

NIGHT FALL

LOCK-IN

JONATHAN MARY-TODD

MINNEAPOLIS

Darby Creek
A division of Lerner Publishing Group, Inc.
241 First Avenue North
Minneapolis, MN 55401 U.S.A.

Website address: www.lernerbooks.com

Cover photographs © iStockphoto.com/dblight (doors);
© iStockphoto.com/Kevin Cooke (handprint).

Main body text set in Memento Regular 12/26.

Library of Congress Cataloging-in-Publication Data
Mary-Todd, Jonathan.
Lock-in / by Jonathan Mary-Todd.
    p.   cm. — (Night fall)
Summary: When a high school lock-in, meant to ease tensions
between the lacrosse team and a group that likes to play
werewolf, goes awry, Jackie does not know if she is safer in the
panic of the dark hallways or with the crazed student council
president determined to maintain control.
ISBN 978-0-7613-7743-6 (lib. bdg. : alk. paper)
[1. Interpersonal relations—Fiction. 2. High schools—Fiction.
3. Schools—Fiction. 4. Werewolves—Fiction. 5. Horror stories.]
    I. Title.
PZ7.M36872Loc 2011
[Fic]—dc22   2011000960

Manufactured in the United States of America
1—BP—7/15/11

For 8th & College
and other small-scale disasters

I shouldn't have been surprised when my friend Francis hit the Internet. As early as sixth grade, he told me he was going to make a splash. He said it the same way he said almost everything, like he was half-kidding and with a grin that showed he knew just how he sounded. But basically I believed him.

About one thousand years later, as a junior, I watched the clip on YouTube for the first time. It started with a reporter from WBNE, our local TV station, talking to a local farmer. Callie Murdock owned land on the edge of

Bridgewater. For weeks, she complained, kids had been stealing her chickens.

"Not even to eat," Callie said. "Just killing 'em sometimes! I found some still on my land. Dead as doornails." She tapped a shovel on the ground for emphasis.

"I know who it is, too," she went on. "Those . . . wolf kids! I've seen 'em around. Just lurkin' near the farm."

The clip cut to the same reporter talking straight to the camera: "For most citizens of Bridgewater, Halloween season ended months ago. But a new trend in the halls of Bridgewater High School finds *some* teens wearing their best werewolf gear each day of the week. Connor Tailors, Mike Sizemore, Gwen O'Gara, and Francis Masterson are at the front of the pack. These Bridgewater High eleventh-graders say it's simple self-expression."

The camera cut to four teens in black jeans and black T-shirts. Gwen faced away from the camera. A fake-fur tail hung from her belt in back.

The camera zoomed in on Connor, the tallest of the group. The close-up revealed his deep-red colored contacts. "We don't think anybody's just, like, human," he said. "We're just letting out the animal parts of ourselves."

For most of the clip, Francis just fiddled with one of the many bracelets on his wrists. But he perked up when the reporter asked about the lost chickens. "When I heard about that, I was as worried as anyone else," he said, totally straight-faced. "It's getting so you can't even cross the road here anymore."

The clip cut to Principal Weston in his office. "Well, there's nothing about tails in the dress code," he chuckled. "As long as they're in their seats and learning, I don't see a problem. These things come and go."

Last time I checked, something like a hundred thousand people had watched the footage. I was shocked at the reaction, and then shocked that I was so shocked. Because again, Francis getting semi-famous? Totally plausible. He was good at putting himself out there. And I guess the wolf thing wasn't something most people saw every day. Worth a click. I think the whole situation was just much dumber than I'd expected.

Nowadays, it's easy to say that I should have taken Connor's words more seriously. Everyone in Bridgewater should have. But back then, I just didn't know. Nobody did.

I don't know if the wolf kids were out for attention. Other than Francis, anyway. But after that video blew up on the YouTubes, they got it. Lots of it.

The clip maybe wasn't great for peer relations at Bridgewater High. Before the wolf kids went viral, things had been tense between them and the lacrosse team. Some name-calling in the hallway. At worst, a pushing match that didn't lead anywhere. All of it seemed . . . not *fun*, but pretty normal. And I guess pack behavior is what you can expect from kids who've decided they're actually, you know, wild animals. Still—things seemed uglier after the clip got so many views.

I tried talking about it with Francis once or twice. He and I had been best friends from age five 'til sometime around the start of high school. No real reason why we drifted apart—I think we both just felt like ninth grade meant we were supposed to go looking for something else. For Francis, it had been drama club, movie club, and then pretending to be half-canine. Anyway, we were still friendly.

"Fwwwwancissss!"

That was Blake Golding, attacker for Bridgewater High Lacrosse.

"You know, Blake, lots of *fascinating* people were named Francis," Francis replied. "Francis Scott Key wrote our national anthem! How 'bout that?" Francis shot Blake a big fake grin and got shoved against his locker. I walked up to him afterwards.

"Seems like that kind of thing has been happening to you a lot lately."

Francis chuckled. "Yeah. I'm thinking about

getting a paw-print tattoo like the one Connor has. Maybe they'll make fun of me for that instead."

Connor Tailors was new to Bridgewater this year. He'd come from somewhere in Michigan and brought the whole wolf thing with him.

"Well, try not to do anything too stupid," I said. "I don't want your next YouTube smash to be you eating a live turkey."

"No promises, Jackie. Everything's gotta be bigger in the sequel."

As Francis headed to class, Student Council President Rosa De La Torre approached me. Unlike Francis, I'd managed never to fall in with a crowd. Freshman year, I tried cross-country for a few weeks. My brother Pete, a year older, had already made varsity. The girls' coach said that anyone from the same gene pool would be a natural. I liked the spaghetti dinners but hated the running. Lately my thing had been updating the student council website. My parents said it'd be good for applying to colleges, and there was no chance of getting shin splints.

Rosa had been upset with me ever since I

put a picture of a Speedo-wearing bodybuilder on the site's homepage. (Explaining the joke— "*Stud.* co.?"—didn't help.) But basically we had a good working relationship. She looked at me and then looked at Francis down at the end of the hall.

"Those emo-werewolf kids give me the *creeps*," Rosa said. "What were you even talking about?"

"Francis is harmless. Some crimes against fashion, maybe, but—"

"I'm just saying, Jackie. You're a part of student council. What you do reflects on people other than you. You need to figure out what kind of image you want people to see."

At the time, I didn't know how right Jackie was. But in not too long, the pressure to choose a side was going to get a lot worse.

A bell rang. I was late to Principles of Physics.

"Understood, Madame President."

For some reason, my mom has an easier time making an event out of dinner if the food comes from another country. Monday night is not potato-salad night, although we almost always have potato salad. But Tuesday nights are Enchilada Nights at the Ballards'.

"You're really wolfing those down tonight, Pete!" Mom said.

Pete was like a whole foot taller than me, and sometimes it seemed like he was twice as skinny. Which I don't know how he pulled off, because every Tuesday he ate like six enchiladas. But again, running was his thing.

My dad took a second to laugh at the joke he was about to make. "Hey, speaking of wolves," he said, "what has Francis gotten himself up to? I saw that video . . ."

"Oh god," I groaned, "I guess that makes everybody."

"Werewolf kids!" Pete said between bites. "Think they're werewolves. I think it's 'cause of *Twilight*."

"Francis says that Connor says he's never seen it," I said. I turned to Dad. "Francis, at least, doesn't think he's a wolf-person. I think he's just happy to find people he can talk about old horror movies with."

"Great enchiladas!" Pete said to Mom, closing out our werewolf talk. "Good Enchilada Night."

Anyone who didn't know Pete might think at first that he was dumb. He really wasn't. He just didn't seem to worry about anything. Cross-country, classes, getting along with people—it all came easy to him.

"These *are* good, hon," my dad said. "They

have some real *bite* to them." I glared at him while he let out another laugh.

I got to school the next day right after the first Big Incident happened. A group of kids were gathered in the parking lot in front of Bridgewater High. A police officer tried shooing them away, which proved sorta worthless. The cop just seemed to attract more kids. Another officer dragged a roll of yellow tape around some parking cones like a nonspeaking character from *C.S.I.* Within the cones, I saw a tiny maroon sedan with its front window busted in.

The window had one huge dent with like a million cracks in it. It was ready to totally fall apart at a touch. Someone had written *AWWWWOOOO!* in shaving cream on the car's hood.

In the inner ring of gawking students, Francis stood with Connor and Gwen O'Gara. Gwen had her hands cupped over her mouth. She looked pale. Like, more pale than those kids usually looked. No way the car was anyone's but hers.

I squeezed toward the wolf kids and called out.

"Francis! What . . ."

"Lacrosse kids," he sighed. "Had to be."

Connor didn't acknowledge me but suddenly spoke to Gwen: "They'll regret this. We'll make them."

The lacrosse guys were not discreet. I should know, I sat behind two of them in Advanced Algebra.

"Todd didn't even mean to break the

windshield!" one said. "Just busted on him while he was writing on the car. He got up on it."

"Man, Todd is an idiot."

"Todd is hil-*ar*-i-ous."

I'm sure it wasn't long until Francis or one of his friends heard the same conversation somewhere else. By the end of the school day, the whole wolf pack was deep into plotting. I passed them after classes ended, taking the long way to the student council room. They were huddled in a semicircle near some vending machines in the back lobby. They looked extra-packlike.

"*Psst!*" I fake-whispered to Francis. "What are you guys talking about?"

He looked over at me and then looked back toward his friends. I decided to pester him for just a second longer.

"*Twilight*? I knew it. No shame in that, man, those are good movies!"

Normally this would have been enough to make Francis snicker like an idiot. But if he was amused, he sure didn't let on. Connor squinted at the both of us.

"Jackie," Francis muttered, "Um, don't you have anywhere to be?"

I started back down the hallway.

I didn't see Francis for the next few days. I spent the weekend solving physics problems and updating member profiles on the student council site. I wasn't sure what he got up to, but after the second Big Incident the following Monday, it was easy to guess.

Normally I ate lunch with Mira Patel, a sophomore I knew from the drawing class we had the hour before. She was way better than I was.

"You should at least *think* about joining the web team, Mira," I urged. "You could do some rad graphics for it."

"I don't know why you spend so much time on that stuff," she said, prodding a piece of carrot cake with her fork.

"Neither do I. But it'd be really great to have someone else around who understands that Rosa De La Torre is insane."

We were on the verge of a breakthrough when shouts erupted at the other end of the cafeteria. (The whole lunch crowd goes silent when a fight starts, which is nice.)

"*Sick*, man!"

Todd Fry, captain, Bridgewater High Lacrosse, was upset. Like really upset. Blake Golding and a few other letter-jackets flanked him on both sides. Todd stood at the head of the table where Francis, Connor, and the other wolf kids sat.

"Chicken guts in our equipment room!? You're *sick*, man!"

Connor looked up at him, glowering. He pushed his bangs to one side and let a grin slip.

"Dunno what you're talking about."

Todd grabbed the rim of Connor's lunch tray and flipped it into the air. Most of the food

actually got on Francis, but in a half-second
Connor was on his feet. The adults supervising
the cafeteria got to the table in a hurry too.
(The Bridgewater High cafeteria is actually a
terrible place to start a fight if you don't want it
broken up right away.)

A couple teachers moved in and separated
Todd and Connor. Mike Sizemore picked up a
cup of Jell-O like he was ready to chuck it, but
he put it back down when Principal Weston
appeared.

Weston asked the teachers to keep the
groups apart and take them to different rooms
in the guidance counselors' office. He walked
through the cafeteria, fuming, toward the exit
on Mira's and my side of the room.

"This isn't going any further," he muttered
to one of the grown-ups placed near the door.
As Weston headed out of the cafeteria, Rosa
stood up a few tables away and moved to follow
him.

"There goes your president," Mira said.
"What do you think she wants?"

"I'm sure she's got a solution to all of this,"
I laughed. "Maybe student council will pay

for lacrosse lessons for the werewolves. And eyeliner for the lacrosse team. Let them walk a mile in the other's paws."

Rosa did have a plan. It should have struck me as crazy right away, but mostly the idea of extra work was what stuck out. Doing web stuff meant I went along mostly unbothered. Rosa insisted on everybody's participation this time, though. It was going to be big, and somehow she got Principal Weston on board.

Connor and Todd were the only ones who got in trouble for the cafeteria thing. Some teachers saw Connor shake his fists and Todd flip the tray, but I guess they couldn't prove anything else, like who messed up Gwen's car the week before. Anyway, I'm sure Principal Weston wanted to do *something* before he started getting swamped with calls from concerned parents. Before Weston made the event official, Rosa filled in student council at our Thursday meeting.

"We're having a lock-in," she announced. "Friday night to Saturday morning, three weeks from now. We'll have trust-building games, student bands—it'll be like a chance to get to know other students for the first time. A fresh start!"

The rest of us mostly looked around at each other. Slightly less enthused.

Macy, the student council treasurer, spoke up. "What about the stuff that's been happening, the fights? Don't we wanna keep some kids, like, as far away from each other as possible?"

Rosa's smile dropped off for a second, then curled back up. "Bridgewater High is a small school. You can't expect people to stop running into each other. Principal Weston and I agree that nothing's going to get fixed until we all try to understand each other a little bit better. We have the administration's full support. But it's up to us to organize it."

At that point, I started to get curious. "Um, I know *I* like trust-building, but how are we gonna get people to actually go?"

Rosa did the smile-frown-smile thing again. "Attendance is mandatory, except for the boys' and girls' basketball teams. They have away games. But everyone gets half their civics credits taken care of just for going. It's like getting credits for going to a party! For kids who still don't attend, the administration will . . . figure something out."

The next couple weeks went by in a flash. All of us in student council kept busy putting together Rosa's Fresh Start Lock-In. It seemed like everybody else was lying low. No more smashed windshields, animal guts, or uncomfortable conversations in the Bridgewater High cafeteria.

Money for the lock-in came from fundraisers earlier in the school year. This was the pile of money that usually went toward school dances. Which the lock-in sort of was, except this time I'd be bored and watching the clock for like four times as long.

I think Rosa spent most of the funds on streamers. No kidding. In the days before the lock-in, I'm pretty sure all I did was put up paper streamers.

For a while the stupid rolls kept running away from me until I figured out how to measure out enough colored tissue paper to cover a distance with a nice, hanging swoop. The worst was when a piece wouldn't be long enough and I had to connect two sections of streamer with a piece of tape midstream. It never looked right.

On the day before Fresh Start Friday, I volunteered to make sure streamers were swooping nicely in the back lobby. I also re-taped any balloons that kids might have punched off the walls. (Tape a balloon in one place and it just begs to be batted away.) Francis was standing there when I finished up interior decorating. He tapped at his phone's keypad.

"Where's the rest of the pack?"

"Connor and Mike are at Connor's house. Gwen gets her car back today. I'm meeting up with them in a few."

Francis's voice was flat. He started to look extra-eager to leave.

"You guys going to the lock-in tomorrow?" I asked. "Or are you too cool? I hear the school will tack on a whole six extra civics credits for no-shows."

Francis didn't respond at first. He avoided my eyes for a few seconds.

". . . Maybe that would be a blessing in disguise though. I volunteered in the computer room at the public library for my civics credits last year and learned a lot. Interesting new curse words from the middle-schoolers playing *World of Warcraft*."

"Jackie. . . . You should . . . just keep away from us tomorrow, all right?"

"What?"

Francis didn't reply.

"I wasn't exactly planning on applying for wolf pack membership," I said. "Bridgewater High Student Council is actually *super* fulfilling."

Francis glared at me.

"I mean it. Stay away."

His phone began to vibrate. He took a quick look at the screen and then left without saying anything else. At some point I had let go of my streamer roll. It came undone as it wobbled along the hallway, leaving a long trail of red tissue paper behind it.

Pete and I drove to the lock-in together in the station wagon Mom and Dad had handed down to him. Pete's a little bit country, and I'm a little bit rock and roll. Like usual, we settled on Ghostface Killah.

"There gonna be food there?" he asked.

"There'll be pizza. Lotta pizza. I think some chips. They're not going to keep us at school for half a day and not feed us."

"You never know."

I thought about explaining why you *would*

know, but I didn't. Pete reached into a cavity on the driver's side door and grabbed part of a bagel.

"Is that the same bagel you were eating this morning?"

"Yup. Didn't finish it."

I looked away while he ate, gazing out the passenger's side window.

"Your cross-country boys gonna be there tonight?"

"Gotta be," Pete said, still chewing. "You know that."

"Yeah," I said. "I'm just sorta surprised that people are actually doing it."

"Francis gonna be there?"

"I dunno. Yeah. Why do you always ask me about him?"

"I dunno." He turned his head my way and raised his eyebrows a few times.

"It was never like that." (It really wasn't!) "We were just good friends. And anyway, we were like nine years old when we hung out. And I'm pretty sure Francis still hasn't kissed a girl."

"Uh huh."

"Having a really good boy friend—like

friend-who-is-a-boy friend—only seems weird 'cause I don't have any girl friends," I said.

"Come on. There's . . . what's her name?"

"Mira? Yeah. Yeah, Mira's cool."

"And at student council . . . you know, the web stuff."

We both paused after that.

"You know, you realize, Pete, you just named student council instead of another human being. You're not disproving my point."

Pete chuckled.

"Well—yeah. You're good at being you, though! You *own* it."

"I do own it."

We looked at each other and both gave a stiff nod. Pete turned up the music.

I honestly did try to enjoy the lock-in once Pete and I got inside. For a while, I even succeeded! I have to admit, all of Rosa's planning paid off. By eight P.M. the Bridgewater High gym was a flurry of activity.

I got in line for a soda and watched the first student band, the Superchiefs, set up their stuff. Macy lined up behind me.

"Are we having fun yet, Macy?"

"You should try the indoor lawn darts. I'm three-and-oh right now."

"Impressive."

"Also, Rosa's looking for you."

I grimaced. "What for? What could she possibly be looking for me for?" I motioned to the waves of streamers along the gym walls. "I put those up! That was my job! They're still up! My job is *over*." I moved to the head of the line. "One root beer, please."

Suddenly Rosa was next to me.

"Hiiii Jackie! Isn't this going great?"

"Yep. Magical."

"I think you did *such* a great job with the streamers and I would not even *think* about asking you to do anything else except Meredith was supposed to work the pizza station and she totally has the flu and I know this is *super* last-minute but it would be *really* awesome of you so do you think you can hand out pizza?"

I felt like I had been tricked somehow.

The view from the pizza station was pretty good when the lines weren't too long. I could watch the trust falls, the lawn darts, the bad dancing. I was supposed to limit students to one piece of pizza, but after the third of my brother's friends tried pleading for two, I gave in completely. The sooner we ran out, the sooner I could leave my station, I figured.

"Pizza, pizza!" I called out. "Extra slices for students with two hands."

On the far side of the gym, I noticed a small cluster of students all staring in the same direction. Not talking. A few seconds later, the students behind them stopped talking and started looking that way too. Soon most of the kids in the gym formed a half-circle around one of the main doorways.

Gradually the swath of kids divided in two. The onlookers formed a pathway as Blake Golding stumbled onto the gym floor. His T-shirt collar was torn, like someone had yanked it hard from one side. One of the sleeves on his letter jacket looked halfway unstitched. His shoulder poked through it with every other step. Todd Fry and a few friends shoved their way through the crowd.

"Blake!" Todd shouted. "Man, what

happened?"

Blake looked up like he was about to reply. His face was a mess of scrapes and scratches.

I stood atop the pizza station table to get a better angle. I noticed a winding trail of blood droplets behind Blake that must have come from the big gash on his cheek. I followed the trail with my eyes back toward the doorway 'til a hard thud broke my concentration. Before Blake managed to speak, he dropped to his knees and fainted outright in the arms of his bros.

I'm still not sure why things happened the way they did after Blake stumbled into the gym. Maybe all of us were sort of like the busted windshield on Gwen's car. One extra push ran through cracks that were already there. And everything burst into pieces.

I don't even know who cut the lights. Could have been one of the meatheads on the lacrosse team. Could've been Connor or Mike. Or it could have been anybody else at the lock-in. If I've learned anything from that night, it's that you never really know what another person is capable of.

Within a minute or two of Blake's collapse, the adults on the scene were all over him with a first-aid kit. Mr. Spragues, one of the guidance counselors, busted open some smelling salts. He and Ms. Anders, another counselor, got Blake up and walking again. The three of them took one of the gym's doorways to the outside so he could get some air. Mr. Brown, one of Bridgewater High's English teachers, got on his cell phone, probably trying to reach the police.

The remaining grown-up, Principal Weston, got up on the pizza table as I lowered myself down. I began stacking empty pizza boxes as he attempted to address the students. Don't ask me why. I was nervous.

"Everybody—may I have your attention. Remain calm. The police—everybody! Please—"

He struggled to be heard over the buzzing of nervous kids. Most students stood facing the inside of whatever clump they were a part of, ignoring the principal.

"We are contacting Sheriff Brady and the rest of the sheriff's department. We're going to make sure things are all right everywhere in the building, and then we're going to get this back underway. In the meantime, we ask that you stay—"

A thought hit me: *Oh god. The freakin' wolf kids.* I scanned the gym. *Francis, where are you?*

"—Those of you who would like to contact your parents—"

He couldn't have, right?

Suddenly the door to the outside slammed shut. Whatever was propping it up must have fallen over. Mr. Brown knocked hard a few times and waved at Weston through the window.

"All right," Weston said, slowly and loudly. He mouthed the words toward the people at the window, dangling a bunch of keys up for them to see. "Coming . . ."

And like that, it all went black. Every light in the gym, in the hallways outside of it—out. People started to scream, run, push. And I'm pretty sure I heard someone knock over my stack of pizza boxes.

A few kids ran to the outside door, but most of the noise traveled into the hallways. Everyone scrambled to keep track of a friend. I think Weston kept shouting stuff, but I doubt he had much of a plan at that point.

I hollered for Pete and got nothing. Someone running by clipped my shoulder, and I lost any sense of where I was. In the dark, no one direction made more sense than another. I bit my lower lip and started to run.

Something, probably a pizza box, took away my footing. I stumbled back. As I fell, a pair of hands seized my shoulders.

"Jackie!"

The light from a cell phone dashed back and forth in front of my face.

"What . . . ?"

The stranger moved the phone away from my eyes. I made out Rosa's up-do in the pale blue light.

"Rosa . . . ?"

"You all right?" she asked.

"Yeah. I think so? Better than Blake. I might have peed a little."

She grabbed my sleeve and started walking.

"Where are we going? Should we take the pizza?"

She gave my arm a jerk. "Where do you think? Student council room." She breathed angry breaths. "They are not taking this night away from me."

Rosa paced back and forth against the student council whiteboard. The power was still out, but she had turned on a laptop. The glow of the screen lit her face like an artificial campfire. Principal Weston sat in a chair by the corner, patting his brow with a handkerchief and generally not looking like the person in charge.

"The police have been called," Rosa said. "Blake's outside. They're coming to get him. It's up to us to make sure that's all they do. We need to show them that there's no reason why this lock-in can't keep going. I'm not going to let some stupid prank ruin our fresh start. I'm not going to let them embarrass me—embarrass *us*, or," she looked at the principal, "the administration."

Macy raised her hand. "Where are the other adults?"

The principal cleared his throat. "The keys were . . . misplaced in, uh, in the panic. I'll let Ms. Anders, Mr. Brown, and Mr. Spragues back in just as soon as the authorities arrive and—"

Macy raised her hand again. "What if this is, like, serious? We don't know why the power isn't working, or—"

Rosa cut him off. "It's a stupid prank by stupid kids!"

She breathed more angry breaths, then lowered her voice back to normal. "All we need to do is let people know it's okay. We've got to be able to show the police that this is under control."

She looked at Weston again. He nodded. Maybe he wasn't sure what else to do.

"Macy. Jackie. First thing, I want you guys to hit the hallways," Rosa said. "Anybody you find, ask them to head back to the gym. We'll go in shifts. We want everyone back in one place, soon."

Macy furrowed her brow. "What if people don't listen? That was scary stuff, what happened."

Rosa turned her laptop around so it shone in Macy's face. "Be *convincing*. And if you see someone has the keys, grab them. We can't get out any easier than people can get in. Principal Weston can't even get the extra pairs in his office. All the doors were locked at the beginning of the—"

"Of the *lock*-in," I said under my breath. "That name makes so much more sense now."

In the faint laptop light, Rosa looked like she was turning a different color.

"And with the power out," she continued, "we need actual keys. No way to get out electronically. Typing in a security code or anything like that won't open the doors."

I looked at Macy and shrugged. I still felt a little shaken from my wipeout on the gym floor, but I figured that the hallway recon party would be safer than staying in the same room as Rosa.

The halls were quiet. Macy and I walked around, knocking on classroom doors and using our phones like flashlights. Student council's room was on the first floor, so we decided to work our way up.

Most kids must have decided to run for high ground. For a while, we got nothing. Eventually, we found a bunch of freshmen I half-recognized sitting on sofas in the faculty lounge. We dutifully told them to go to the gym. They nodded but didn't move to get up.

"This is so dumb," Macy said. I nodded. "I mean it," she continued. "I'm getting out of here. I'll figure out a way. Rosa can yell at me later."

"Well, then she can yell at both of us," I replied. "I'm not going back by myself."

We took a turn away from the next row of classrooms and walked in the direction of the front entrance. Macy fumbled around her pockets for her car keys. As we neared the end of the main hallway, I stopped walking.

"Macy! I'm not sure we're taking off anytime soon."

Somebody—some group of people—had taken three teacher's desks from elsewhere in the building. They stood blocking the path to the front doors like barricades, keeping us from reentering the outside world.

Macy grabbed the underside of one of the desks. She grunted and tried to lift. It didn't budge.

"It must have taken like five guys to get that here before."

She glared at me. "You wanna help?"

"So I can get a hernia?" I asked. "Come on, let's get back to student council. They actually probably need to know this."

Macy and I stated to sort of run-walk back. Running would have been like admitting we were really starting to worry.

"I've heard of lock-ins, but this is ridiculous!" I said. I gave her a fake grin but she didn't smile back. And, like, what I said wasn't that funny, but normally she'd at least have been polite. We were really starting to worry.

Two steps sounded out somewhere in the hall behind us as we approached the back lobby. Light and sudden, like a *click-click.* The noise stopped before we turned around.

"Hello?"

Nothing. The halls looked empty.

"Um, it's student council?" That sounded weird. "Hello? It's Jackie? Ballard. Jackie Ballard. You probably don't—we're asking people to go back to the gym? If you see people—"

Macy started walking again. "There's nobody there."

"Well then what was that?"

Click-click.

We turned back around but saw no signs of movement. Another *click* sounded against the tile floor, this time in the back lobby.

Macy tapped my shoulder as if to say, "Wait here." She headed into the lobby.

"Who's there?"

The back lobby was a big, baseball-diamond-shaped space with three entrances: the middle hallway that Macy and I had just walked, a hall to the right that led to the student council room, and a hall to our left that led to the library and a few classrooms. Macy took a few steps to the right and squinted down the corridor. The clicks started again, faster, one after another. Like nails on linoleum.

"Jackie, run."

Macy seemed to freeze in place as I moved. A black mass lunged at her, and she folded at the waist. Her body hit the tiles with a *smack*, the darkness right on top of her. I ran left without looking back. A long howl followed me down the hallway over my panicked, heavy breaths.

I slammed the library's double doors behind me and rested my back against them, panting. My knees buckled and I slid slowly down 'til I was a pile on the floor.

All right. Gasp. *What just happened?*

It took several breaths before I realized I wasn't alone.

"Get out of here!" someone shouted.

I looked up. Whoever had said it didn't seem to be yelling at me.

"I mean it! Get out of here! We were here first!"

Two groups of kids, like eight or nine apiece, stood on opposite sides of the library. Several bookshelves separated them. Through the moonlight that shone in the library's large windows, I recognized the speaker. Albert Sciuto ran the Bridgewater High Computer Club. We'd asked him for help a couple of times when serious website problems popped up. A kid on the other side shouted back at him.

"What do you mean you were here first?" The boy wore dark-rimmed glasses and a turtleneck sweater. He pointed to a sheet of banner-sized paper taped to the wall behind him. It said *Bridgewater High Poets' Society* in thick, marker-written cursive letters. "We meet here every Thursday!"

"Today is not Thursday!" Albert said. "We. Got. Here. First! Find somewhere else to camp!"

A hardcover book went sailing past Albert's head.

"How dare—"

The next one hit him in the face. Members of the computer club began pulling books off the shelves and hurling them across the library. The poets did the same. A tall, heavyset computer clubber picked up a dictionary and flung it. He knocked down a frail-looking girl who'd mostly been dodging books.

"For Ginsberg, for Dickinson, for Sylvia P!" the boy in the turtleneck cried.

"Long live the Bridgewater Poets' Society!" the rest of the poets shouted in response.

Book after book flew in an arch over the stacks. Once in a while, two hit in midair and pages flew out like feathers.

I tried creeping toward a corner on the computer club side. Without even looking in my direction, Albert pointed at me and shook his head "no." The tall guy moved to stand in my way, arms folded.

I backed off and stared down the center of the library. It was a straight shot to the doors on the other end. The only things in my way were the reference books being thrown like shot puts. I pulled up the hood of my sweatshirt and got moving.

I made it out of the library bruised but basically unharmed. No contact with sharp corners or any dictionary-sized items. I felt a book bang against the library door after I slammed it shut behind me.

I'd sort of assumed that some of the computer clubbers were filled with pent-up rage, but the poetry club too? What was going on? I thought of Macy, then of Blake Golding. How many more kids were going to get mangled before the police found a way in?

The sound of books landing and the occasional chant from the poets bled through the door. I took a step forward, but I could barely make anything out in the dark. A row of lockers stood a few feet in front of me. Somewhere nearby were the weight rooms and the training room where I'd gotten my shins taped up during my cross-country days. A whole side hallway of athletic-type rooms outside the gym, close to the library. But there was no telling if I'd be any safer there.

Maybe I can track down some Icy-Hot to squirt at my next attempted murderer, I thought. *Crap. I am really, dangerously alone right now.*

Over the noise from the library, I began to hear footsteps down the hall. Not like the last time—louder, more rhythmic. More than one pair, not afraid to let you know they were coming. Suddenly they were upon me.

"You waiting on anyone in particular, Jackie?" asked one of the steppers.

"Pete!"

"Are you okay?"

"Still breathing," I said. "Almost lost my life in a hurricane of nerd rage."

"What?"

"Don't go into the library."

I leaned up against a locker and breathed a sigh of relief.

"Pete—" I started, not really knowing what to ask. "What are people doing?"

"The school's gone crazy. Far as I can tell. We went looking for you."

He nodded to the two cross-country guys who had run up alongside him. "Carl's got a little sister somewhere in the building too. Cross-country's managed to occupy the wrestling room. It's comfortable—mats on the floors. A good place to camp out until stuff stops being so weird."

"Only one door in or out," he added. "Easy to defend."

I cocked an eyebrow.

"So there's no way to escape if a bunch of rabid creative writers try to storm it?" I asked. "That sounds great, Pete."

He folded his arms. "Are you coming or not?"

One of his teammates spoke up: "We gotta keep moving, Pete."

I grabbed an ankle and tried to stretch. "I'm in, I'm in! Of course I'm in."

We took off running, Pete's two friends in front, me straggling behind. Pete hung in the middle, shooting me concerned glances every few steps.

I couldn't remember running so much in one day since quitting cross-country as a freshman. My lungs kept trying to take in new breaths before I managed to breathe out the previous ones. I forced my knees up in sloppy jerking motions. But I might as well have been running in place. The gap between me and the guys in front got wider and wider.

After a few turns, I stopped completely and leaned over. Panting, I gripped the edges of my thighs. Every muscle felt like it was tightening up.

Pete jogged back to where I'd quit. "Come on, Jackie, let's keep moving."

I tried to steady my breathing before I replied. "You don't think here's good? I think here's good." I coughed. "How do you guys deal with all this lactic acid?"

"I'm serious, Jack, we can't stay here."

The guys up ahead were barely visible in the dark up ahead. Their footsteps halted for a sec.

"Pete, we can't stop again!" one of them shouted. "We said no stopping."

Pete grabbed my sleeve and spoke with a kind of sternness I wasn't used to. "Jackie—"

"I can't keep up," I gasped.

Pete sighed, quickly and quietly. He called out to the guys ahead: "Just keep going! We'll . . . be all right."

My stomach sank as their footsteps got farther away. I tried to work back into a slow jog.

"I gave one of those jerks extra pizza, you know."

"Just keep moving, Jackie. Follow me."

We started up a nearby stairwell to the second floor.

"Where are we going?" I whispered. "I thought we were going to the wrestling room."

"We *were* going to the wrestling room," Pete said. "You stopped running. Now I want to find the closest open classroom or broom closet or something and hole up in it. It's not safe out here."

"You know something I don't, Pete?"

"If you don't keep it down, you're gonna attract unwanted attention."

"Fine!" I hissed. "But you better know that I take that as a *yes*."

We did find a broom closet at the top of the stairs. I knocked over a couple of spray bottles on the way in, but no one seemed to be wandering the second-floor hallway. Nobody came pounding at the closet door, anyway.

"Sooo," I started. "Now we wait?"

"Yep," Pete replied. "We wait."

I got Pete to reveal the bit he knew that I didn't. He said a couple cross-country guys had a bad run-in with some lacrosse types. Like the team was looking to get payback for Blake from anybody close enough to blame. I guess he hadn't wanted to make me more worried than I was already.

"Are we going to be Bridgewater High's two remaining students tomorrow morning?" I asked.

"We're going to be fine. This can't last forever, whatever it is. Where are your wolf-friends, by the way?"

"No idea." I slapped my cheek. "Oh god. But Pete, when Macy and I were walking the halls earlier—"

Pete stopped me. "Wait. Jack, do you hear that?"

"Hear what?"

"Listen. That sort of . . . thumping."

We both stayed quiet for a minute.

"Pete. That sounds like a . . . bass line."

"Weird."

We were quiet again for a sec.

"Weird?" I asked. "That's all? It can't be bad, can it? Someone, somebody nearby is playing music."

"We're staying here," he said.

"We *have* to check this out."

"We're staying here."

"This could mean the worst is over!" I said.
"You enjoy the mops. I'm checking it out."

I followed the sound a few doors down the
hallway. Pete followed behind me, watching
both our backs. We stopped outside the art
room.

"It's coming from here," I said.

I slid the door open a crack and peered
inside. I have no idea how long I looked for. But
afterward, I gently closed the door and frowned.

"Well, what?" Pete asked. "What did you
see?"

"I hate this night. Just when I thought it
couldn't get weirder."

Inside the art room, kids were playing
music from the speakers of a laptop. A couple
pounded on the lids of sealed paint cans.
Others danced on top of tables. Mira Patel, one
of the few I recognized, held a large flashlight.
She kept flicking it on and off like it was a
strobe. During the bursts of light, I could see

that paint had been splashed throughout the room. Maybe by the canful. A few kids had smeared it over their clothes and faces.

"Jackie, what is going on in there?"

"I'm not sure. I think it might be art."

Pete nudged me away from the door and took a look. The kids either continued not to notice us or they didn't care.

"I have no idea what I'm looking at," he said.

I shrugged.

Pete pointed to Mira. "You know her, right?"

"Yeah," I said. "Mira Patel. You want me to talk to her?"

"I . . . think so? I guess they're not fighting each other. It looks roomier than the broom closet."

I approached Mira at the center of the room, weaving through dancing kids. Pete stayed as close to the door as possible.

"Mira!"

She looked at me blankly.

"We were just passing through, and we wondered if maybe—"

She motioned for me to stop talking.

"I'll ask," she said. "I'll see what I can do."

Mira walked over to two kids who were at the laptop, probably working on the playlist. I couldn't hear what they were saying over the music, and I could barely make out their gestures as long as Mira pointed her flashlight at the ground.

Mira moved back toward me and held the flashlight up to her face. She wore a look of disappointment. Or pity.

"Jackie. I'm sorry."

"What?"

"You have to go."

"Excuse me?"

"You can't stay here, Jackie. I did what I could. You're—," she took a deep breath. "You're just not cool enough."

I wasn't sure how to reply. Mira pointed the flashlight toward me, holding it out.

"Here," she said. "Take this."

"Um, thanks?"

I trotted over to Pete, flashlight in hand. We headed out into the hall, back toward our broom closet.

Back among the cleaning supplies, I was getting bored fast. Pete and I stood in silence. My body felt limp. My muscles still ached from all the running. Pete kept falling asleep and then waking back up once his chin dropped near to his chest.

After a while, a harsh clang shook him awake completely. The clangs traveled our way from the other end of the hall. Something beating on lockers. Soon they sounded only steps away.

"Hey Todd—I think it's clear, man."

"You wanna move one floor down?"

I recognized the voices. The lacrosse players from my math class. Todd Fry had to be with them.

"Yeah," Todd replied. "Yeah, let's go."

I tried standing extra still. I didn't even want to know whether or not they'd crashed the art kids' party.

"We really sent those weirdoes scrambling, right Todd?" asked one of the guys who was not Todd.

I gulped.

"Man, I think I got paint on my shoes," said the other guy who was not Todd.

"Who cares, man?"

"These are new shoes! *T.I.* wears these shoes. You don't like these shoes?"

"I didn't say I didn't—"

Another clang against a nearby locker.

"Shut up, guys," Todd spat. He paused. "You wanna clean your shoes? There's gotta be something in there."

I squeezed my flashlight tight and hoped that hadn't meant what I thought it meant. The door to the closet clicked open. The guy who opened the door immediately grabbed onto my wrist and yanked me out. Pete tried to pull me away, and the other two got on him. He wriggled around trying to get free, but Todd and his buddy each held tight to one of Pete's arms. It took them a second to recognize us in the dark.

"We ran across some of your boys earlier, Pete," Todd said. "They didn't make out so good."

"Let her go!" Pete shouted.

"Don't do it," Todd said to the dude holding me. He turned to the other guy holding Pete. "You got a grip on him? I'm gonna grab my stick."

"Yeah," the guy replied. He put Pete in something like a bear hug. Todd picked up a lacrosse stick a few feet away.

"This isn't personal, Pete," Todd started. "I've seen you race. It's good stuff. But we've gotta show people that no one messes with Bridgewater High Lacrosse. When we're unhappy, everybody's unhappy."

Todd lifted up his stick and twirled it

around a few times. He steadied his feet and raised it behind his head. I thought I heard a faint *click-click*-ing far down the hall.

"You're a jerk!" I shouted. He paused in surprise. I kept at it: "You don't have any right to do this! Not because Blake got beat up. Not because everyone goes to football games but no one goes to yours. You're just a jerk!"

"You're next," Todd muttered.

But I had stalled for long enough. A black mass, like from before, took Todd off his feet. His lacrosse stick went skittering across the floor. Todd's friend loosened his grip on me. I hit him in the knee with my flashlight just in case and ran over to Pete.

"Jackie!"

I turned my head. "Francis?"

Francis jogged up. Gwen and Mike were with him. I clicked on my light.

"Francis, where've you been?"

Todd collided with a wall of lockers. The thing had thrown him, hard. I shined the light on Francis. He did not look happy to see me.

"Jackie," he whispered. "Pete. *Get out of here.*"

Todd smacked back up against the lockers. I turned the light toward the noise, but Francis covered it with his hand.

"Go!"

With everything that had happened so far, I decided to take him at his word. I tugged at Pete's shirt and took a step toward the stairway. But the dark mass stepped into my path. I flashed my light upward.

The thing looked back at me with cold eyes, red like rubies. The shape of its face was human, but black fur lined its cheeks, chin and forehead. The bridge of its nose bulged forward—a snout. Black bangs hung down over its brow.

Connor?

I tried to move underneath its outstretched arms. He caught me by the throat with a strong, hairy hand.

"No," he snarled. "You too."

"**N**o one's going anywhere." Connor's wolflike nostrils flared. The lacrosse guys that came along with Todd lined up against the wall without Connor asking. I dropped my flashlight, and it rolled across the floor. I couldn't see anything of Francis, his friends or my brother in the darkness.

"Francis," I heard Pete say, "What is this?" Gwen and Mike snickered.

"We're everything we said we were," Connor growled. "We're wolves."

Gwen and Mike stepped across the flashlight's beam toward Connor. As they moved, their shadows seemed to grow larger. They were changing too.

"Why are you . . . ?" I wheezed.

"Blake had to pay," Gwen said, her voice lower, scratchier.

"After that, it's just the thrill of the hunt," Mike added.

"But you can fix this!" Pete pleaded. "All the fighting—you can get everybody back to normal!"

Connor laughed. It sounded like a lawnmower starting. "You don't get it. The rest of this, the fighting—that's not me. All it took was a few whiffs of danger for everyone to go running to their packs. I couldn't stop it if I wanted to. It's like I told that dumb reporter: we've all got an animal inside of us." He laughed again. "I'm just better than most people at bringing it out."

One of the lacrosse guys spoke up. "We had no idea about the car thing, man. *No idea.*" Gwen barked and he shut up.

Connor turned back toward me. The

claws at the ends of his fingers dug into my shoulders. "This is pretty perfect timing, actually."

"Francis!" he snarled. "You been having fun tonight?"

Francis didn't reply. How much had he known?

Connor continued: "I think it's time you took the next step. I mean it's about time, right? A pretty perfect way to show your loyalty."

Francis's voice sounded weak. "Jackie," he said. "I didn't know—"

"Come on, Francis," Connor said. "I told you tonight was gonna be big for us. I'm sure you suspected something."

Gwen laughed. "What did you think happened to all those chickens?"

"Tonight's the night you turn, Francis," Connor said. "It's not so bad. Gwen and Mike will tell you—not bad at all."

"All it takes is one little bite," Gwen added.

I started to shake. *A perfect way to show your loyalty.* Starting life as werewolf by taking chunks out of me and Pete.

Francis stammered, barely getting his words out. The werewolf thing really had been a surprise for him too. Maybe cool to see at first. But he sounded as scared of changing as I was of the animal in front of me.

"I'm not . . . I can't."

Gwen and Mike stood between Pete and the lacrosse twins, keeping guard. Francis was on the outside of our cluster of people. He had the open hallway to his back. In my head, I urged him to run. But he just froze.

One the opposite side of the cluster, a lump of Todd Fry shifted in the faint light from a window at the top of the stairs. Todd grabbed hold of the stairway's bottom rail.

"Connor," I blurted, "Looks like your prize chicken's getting away."

He snarled and let go of me. "Watch her!" he shouted, and took his first leap toward Todd. A wave of light zigzagged along some lockers. Francis had picked up the flashlight. He hurled it a few steps in front of Connor. As Connor bounded toward Todd, he slipped on the flashlight's round handle. I heard the head of the light shatter and everything went dark again. *Click-click-clicks* rang against the floor as Connor tried to get his footing back before crashing into the stairway rail. He let loose an angry howl.

I sprinted in Francis's direction, Pete right ahead of me. We ran with no idea where we were headed next. Behind us, I heard shouts and grunts from the lacrosse guys we'd left behind. They tussled with wolf-Gwen and wolf-Mike in the blackness.

I'd like to think the guys took a stand. That they tried to hold back the wolves as Pete, Francis, and I ran. Maybe they tried running themselves and just bumped into Gwen and Mike right away. I felt bad in either case. But as I darted off, ignoring any pain, I understood that I could only focus on one thing from then on: surviving.

"Let's get this straight," I said. "How many werewolves are actually roaming the school right now?"

Pete, Francis, and I had found our way into the kitchen attached to the Bridgewater High cafeteria. We sat on the floor next to industrial-size ovens and steel countertops, back to using phones as flashlights.

"What do you mean?" Francis asked.

"I mean Blake, Macy, I don't know who else. They all got attacked."

"Yeah, but not *bitten*. They got clawed, roughed up. But it takes a bite to get turned."

"Well, I guess *that's* a relief." With my life not in immediate danger, I felt a little more okay with being mad at Francis. "Roughed up? As in not dead?"

"They . . . Connor didn't kill 'em. I don't think he's—"

"You don't think he's a killer?" I asked. "This is all, like, not that comforting."

"Well I didn't know!" Francis yelled. "I knew Connor was weird! I had a feeling Gwen and Mike knew more than I did! But I would have thought twice about hanging with them if I knew that Connor was trying to turn his friends into monsters."

He breathed out, annoyed.

"I'm here now, aren't I?"

"So what, Francis? Am I supposed to thank you for not eating my guts? I'll do that right after I've thanked the other six billion people on Earth for also not eating my guts."

"I'm sorry you don't have many friends, Jackie."

"This is *not. Even. About. That!*"

Pete rubbed his temples and spoke very quietly. "If you two don't shut up, we are definitely going to get found."

I got up to walk to another part of the kitchen. After a few steps, I turned back around.

"Can I ask about the full moon thing?"

"Huh?"

"Like, it's not a full moon tonight, right?" I asked. "Don't werewolves need the light of the moon or something?"

"I don't think it works that way," Francis said. "It's more like they control it by willpower. Sort of like the Green Lantern."

"What?"

"Never mind."

"I hate this night so much right now," I said.

I began to pace around. My stomach growled. I hadn't eaten anything since the lock-in started. Not even the pizza that Rosa made me serve. I looked around on shelves and cabinets before pulling down bags of tortillas and a huge sixty-four-ounce can of black beans. I took a large skillet off the wall and splashed some vegetable oil in it.

"Who wants quesadillas?" I asked.

"No power, Jack," Pete muttered. "Electric stove. Try it. Won't work."

I frowned and took a bite of cold tortilla. Francis sat on a countertop, pushing buttons on his phone.

"Francis," I said between chews, "Who could you possibly be texting right now? 'Cause I know we've been over this, but most of your friends are busy trying to kill us."

"I'm not texting. I'm tweeting."

"You're *tweeting*."

"Since that clip on the news, I've had a bunch of followers," he said. "It keeps my mind occupied. Plus, I've tweeted some very nice things about you. 'Jackie's keeping it together.'"

"I'm speechless, Francis. This is the dumbest thing in the world."

"I didn't actually tweet that."

Pete buried his face in his hands.

The pots and pans hanging on the kitchen walls trembled slightly. Pete lifted his head up. "Someone's coming," he whispered.

The kitchen door burst open before he finished his sentence. Connor, Gwen, and Mike. Fully wolfed-out.

"You didn't think you could hide, did you?" Connor growled. He let out a lawnmower laugh. "Sense of smell, remember?"

Pete stood up and grabbed a large baking tray—the kind you can fit thirty cookies on. He moved slowly toward Connor. Gwen and Mike took to all fours and stepped in front of their leader.

"It's all right," Connor said. "Let him come."

Pete swung the tray with both hands. Connor ducked and swiped at Pete with one paw, then another. Pete hopped back. Gwen and Mike moved in circles around the fighters.

We all watched as Connor lunged at Pete's

throat. Pete blocked the attack with his tray. It wobbled from the impact. Connor yelped and gripped his paw.

"I can do this all night, corndog," Pete said. "Cross-country training."

I have no idea where he got *corndog* from. I am funnier than my brother.

Connor made another pounce and knocked the tray from Pete's hands. Pete doubled back, yanking ladles and spatulas from hooks on the wall and chucking them at the wolf. Connor batted them away with ease. He charged teeth-first at one of Pete's arms.

I reached for my abandoned skillet. "Hey Connor," I shouted, "Eat hot oil!"

I swung the skillet overhand. Vegetable oil drifted through the air, landing in droplets on Connor's fur.

He cringed, expecting to feel the burn. For a moment, no one moved. Connor cautiously opened his eyes, confused. Francis, meanwhile, had grabbed the sixty-four-ounce can of beans. He huffed and tossed it underhand to Pete, who brought it down on Connor's head. Connor crumpled on the floor.

"Holy crap!" I shouted. "Knockout!"

"You *beaned* him, Pete!" Francis hollered.

"Good one," I whispered.

Gwen and Mike barked in anger. Their tails stuck out straight behind them. Mike stalked toward Pete. Gwen turned to me and Francis, baring her fangs. I looked to the walls, but there was nothing left to throw. The wolves advanced, herding the three of us together. In a corner of the kitchen, with no escape plan, I gripped Pete and Francis's hands.

"Guys," I said. From there I meant to say something really meaningful, but instead I threw up a bit of tortilla in my mouth.

Gwen and Mike arched back and prepared to pounce. A small rubber ball sailed through the air and pelted Gwen in the back of the head. She and Mike jerked around. The lacrosse team swarmed through the door and into the kitchen. They wore full protective gear and beat their sticks against the countertops like cavemen in Under Armour.

"I never thought I'd be happy to see a lacrosse player," Francis exclaimed shakily.

"I am so sick of things flying across rooms and hitting other things," I replied. "I'm gonna have nightmares. Just about that."

Todd Fry entered the room with defenders to protect him on both sides. "No mercy, boys!" he shouted.

They weren't in the kitchen to help us. But they weren't coming after us, either. To the lacrosse guys, I don't think it mattered that we were there. They clumped into two waves of five or six, each wave focused on one of the wolves.

Gwen hopped up on a large table in the center of the room. She took a few quick bounds and leapt off, knocking over two of the athletes. They seemed to land okay with all the padding. Gwen held their helmets against the ground, claws hooking around the grids across their facemasks. Mike charged at ground level toward some of the other guys. Sticks clattered and the wolves howled.

Pete, Francis, and I moved along the kitchen wall. We took turns stepping over Connor. He had slowly shifted back to human form after getting knocked out. He lay on the kitchen floor, clothes stretched out from the transformation. A lacrosse stick went flying above me and hit a shelf over my head.

"Do you see what I mean?" I shouted.

We quickened our pace.

As we neared the exit, Mike turned our way. He shook off the three guys wrestling with him and made a final lunge at us. The lacrosse players grabbed his hind legs and pulled him back. He snapped his jaws and glared at Francis, the last one of us to leave.

We ran and kept running. We headed for as far away from the cafeteria kitchen as we could get. I felt like I could run three cross-country races back to back. I moved fueled by pure relief.

The sky outside looked purple whenever we passed by a window. Grapefruit-colored ripples lined the horizon. The sun was rising.

I checked the time on my phone. 4:45 A.M.

"Think the police are here yet?" Pete wondered aloud.

"They could have gotten here hours ago," I said. "But they would have needed a locksmith tagging along with them. And a battering ram to get through the front hallway."

We retraced our steps. We figured that if nothing else, there might be the fewest surprises that way. The art room was empty. Splotches of dry paint covered the floor and the walls. A laptop lay broken in the center of the room. Its screen had snapped off of its body.

Further down the hallway, the door to the janitor's closet was still open wide from when Pete and I got pulled out. Mop handles and spray bottles were scattered on the ground.

We hesitated before moving through the library. But I heard nothing—silence—when I put my ear to the door. We crept inside.

A few dozen books lined the carpet, but at first glance I didn't see anyone around. Then, as we tiptoed through, it drifted through the library: snoring. Francis and I peeked through the stacks as Pete watched behind us. Kids slept quietly on the floor. Computer clubbers and poets alike! They used sweatshirts, backpacks, and in one case the *Encyclopedia Britannica* as pillows. We left through the library's opposite end, taking care not to disturb them.

It wasn't normal. But it made me feel like things were getting back to normal. I didn't know it at the time, but a week later, the Bridgewater High Poets' Society would publish a poem of apology in the school paper.

Occasionally during our run from the kitchen, we'd glance through the window of a classroom door and see students inside. Most of the time they were sleeping, like the kids we saw in the library—kids who had been lucky enough to miss the wolves or a lacrosse thrashing. Who probably even had fun during their lawless night locked up inside the school.

Once we arrived in the back lobby, we weren't sure where to go. Pete took a short jaunt down the main hallway and found that large desks still blocked the front entrance. I looked down the corridor that led to the student council room and felt a pang of guilt.

"Guys," I said, "Let's try this way."

We entered to see that most of the stud. co. kids had nodded off as well. Rosa was nowhere in sight, but Principal Weston still sat in the corner. Our footsteps shook him from his slumber. He started on a drowsy explanation of the last several hours.

"I said 'no more kids out' after you two didn't come back," he started. "She has got such a temper, that girl." Pretty safe to assume he was talking about Rosa. "I've been in touch with the police." Weston rubbed his eyes. "Should be coming in anytime now. Working on ways to open the locks."

"Rosa," I started. "Where is she?"

"Went to the gym," he said, fighting a yawn. "Said she wanted to start cleaning up."

I felt that pang of guilt again. "Guys," I said, turning to Pete and Francis. "I'm going to head over there. Lend her a hand."

"No way, Jackie," Pete replied. "We still don't

know that it's safe around here. My thinking is, we—"

I hushed him and motioned to the windows. Sunlight was beginning to really come through, bold orange waves of it. "Look outside, Pete. It's over. You take a load off—I'm gonna go do my duty as a good student council member."

He winced but didn't argue. "You stay away from the cafeteria," he said. "Just in case."

Francis pretended to cry over the exchange. I stuck my tongue out at him.

"If you die this late in the game, it's totally your own fault," he said. We both grinned.

Rosa had her work cut out for her. In the growing daylight, the gymnasium looked like a freakin' mess. Spilled drinks, torn-up decorations, a busted lawn dart set. Scattered empty pizza boxes that were definitely not my fault. So much junk all over the gym's polished hardwood floor that I didn't know where to start. But where was Rosa De La Torre?

I skipped across the empty cups and soda puddles, glancing left and right.

"Rosa!" I called out. "Um, clean-up crew's here?"

My voice echoed throughout the empty gym. No reply. Did she go back to the student council room? I had taken the long way to the gymnasium, going around the library—we could have missed each other.

I walked onto the small stage where the Superchiefs had played a couple songs. "Gonna count to ten, Rosa!" I called out, sort of to her but mostly to myself. "Then I'm going to . . ." I trailed off and sat myself behind the band's drum set. I took an extra look around and then tapped the bass drum pedal a few times with my foot. I didn't really know what to do from there. I do not know how to play the drums.

I flicked one of the cymbals with my index finger, heard it *ding*, and felt a microphone cord wrap around my neck. I tried to pry it off me but it only got tighter. With sudden force, something dragged me off the chair and onto the ground.

I looked up, and my eyes met Rosa's. "Deserter!" she spat. "You've betrayed student council! You betrayed *me*!"

I tried to speak, to give Rosa one of many reasons why it wasn't really fair of her to strangle me to death, but nothing came out. The microphone cord stayed tight around my neck.

"No one ever says thank you!" she screamed. "People like you—you're supposed to get it. And all you do is sneer!" Her hair was frazzled, her eyeliner smudged.

I kicked, blindly, and hit her ankle. She fell to one knee and lost her grip on the cord.

I whipped it off my head and staggered back, gasping for oxygen. Still dazed, I tripped over the chair behind the drum set, knocking half the set over in the process. Rosa stood up and leaned over me.

"I am sick of doing so much for this school and getting nothing in return," she said coldly.

"At least this'll look great on" *cough* "a college application," I muttered. "That's what it's all about anyway, right?"

Rosa's eyes bulged. "I am not. Just. *Résumé building*!" she shrieked.

She reached to the ground for the drum set's hi-hat, two small cymbals on the top of a metal stand. She swung it like an axe a couple feet in front of me. I grabbed hold of a large cymbal on the ground next to me as Rosa geared up for another swing. She brought the hi-hat down against my makeshift shield. The harsh clang ran through my ears. She brought it down again, just missing a few of my fingers.

Rosa's third swing was so forceful that she doubled back upon impact. I wrapped my hand around a leg on the drum-set chair and whipped it in her direction. She dropped the hi-hat to avoid it, and I managed to get up on my feet. As Rosa dodged the chair, a chain full of keys fell from her pocket.

"The keys!" I shouted. "You—you took Principal Weston's keys!"

"I had to!" she replied. "Don't you see? It was the only way to save the lock-in. I couldn't let people leave. Couldn't let the police in. We had to fix it ourselves . . ."

"No one fixed anything, Rosa! The school broke into pieces last night! Our treasurer got beat up by werewolves! Do you know how much fighting you could've prevented if you'd unlocked those doors?"

Rosa trembled, legs locked, arms shaking. Staring into her eyes, I saw one last thing snap. She ran at me, weaponless, but with a fury that would have made the wolves jealous. I held my cymbal up between me and Rosa, clinging tight. She gripped the top of the rim, between my hands, and pulled the cymbal her way. The tug-of-war lasted for what felt like minutes. Finally my legs began to give out, too weak from the strain of the night.

Rosa yanked the cymbal away and knocked me over with a shove. I fell against the stage. She advanced and kneeled down above me, keeping my arms pinned with her legs. She raised the cymbal over my head—rim first.

"Bridgewater High *will* remember me!" she shouted. Which would be a really terrible last thing to hear.

"Put the cymbal down!" A voice I didn't recognize. Rosa did not move to decapitate me, but she didn't let go right away either. "Put it down, young lady. Now!"

I titled my head. Sheriff Brady ran across the gym with a couple deputies behind him. Principal Weston trailed at the back.

Finally.

Rosa slowly let the cymbal slip from her hands and roll off the stage. The rage drained from her face. As the police got closer, she just looked . . . confused. Her eyes widened as she noticed Principal Weston.

"My transcript," Rosa whispered. "Principal Weston! Will this appear on my transcript?"

The deputies walked up to her. Seeing that the fight had left her, they gently raised her to her feet and guided her off the stage. I don't think she even noticed as they slipped on her handcuffs.

"Will this appear on my transcript?" she asked again. It sounded more like a hushed chant than a question. "Will this appear on my transcript?"

I continued to lie on the stage, staring at the ceiling.

"Are you all right, miss?" the sheriff asked.

"Ready for bed," I replied.

Pete and I sat on the hood of our station wagon, waiting for Mom or Dad to pick us up. He hadn't lost his keys or anything during the night, but the police were insisting that parents or guardians come by for their kids. I pulled a little at the bandage around my neck, trying to loosen it.

Paramedics in the parking lot loaded some kids into a couple of ambulances. They lifted Macy in on a stretcher and then helped up the poor girl from the poets' society who got hit with a dictionary. Police officers sat in one of the ambulances, keeping watch over a few students in cuffs.

Word spread around the lot that the sheriff's department found Gwen and Mike banged up and knocked out (and human-shaped) inside the cafeteria kitchen. A bunch of lacrosse players too, either unconscious or woozy from the lumps they'd taken. I guess neither side made out too well.

From the sound of it, Connor was missing—gone from the kitchen before any grown-ups got there. Maybe he had headed for the woods. But how far could he really get? It's a long way back to Michigan. Anyway, I'm sure the police have tracking dogs for stuff like that. Not runaway werewolves specifically. But stuff-that-has-escaped. My stomach rumbled. I decided to stop worrying and think about hash browns. A mountain of hash browns.

"Look," Pete said, motioning toward the school's front doors, "Todd's coming out."

Todd Fry and Sheriff Brady walked down the stairs of the entryway, Todd in handcuffs. He looked bruised and tired in the light, but he was walking okay. Brady guided him into the back of a squad car.

Francis trotted toward me and Pete, clutching some of the hot chocolate that a few worried parents were handing out in paper cups.

"What do you think this means for next week's lacrosse game?" he said.

Pete rolled his eyes.

"How long you gonna keep that tail on for, Francis?" I asked.

Francis jerked his head and tried to look behind him. Like, literally almost started chasing his fake-fur tail. He grabbed around for the back of his belt and plucked the tail off.

"Let's pretend I never wore that."

"It's on film," I reminded him. "Check YouTube."

He pulled his phone out of his pocket and spent a second staring closely at its screen.

"Just getting bigger and bigger," he said. "I got so many re-tweets after I started talking about the big fight in the kitchen! I think I'm gonna start a video blog too. Maybe my own online magazine . . ."

I noticed my dad in his car at the back of a long line of parents waiting to reach the Bridgewater High parking lot.

"We can give you a ride if you need one," I said. "You have anybody on the way?"

"I think I'm probably sticking around here for a while," he said. "I was with the wolves for a big part of last night." He sighed. "I'm sure the police are going to want to talk to me eventually."

"But you didn't do anything," Pete replied.

"I didn't turn into a wolf and attack anybody," Francis corrected him. "But—I don't know. There's a lot I didn't do to *help* people, too. Whether I'm in trouble is up to the sheriff, I guess."

Dad honked from the side of the road and gestured for me and Pete to come his way. Francis waved good-bye and headed back toward the school. Pete and I began to walk across the stretch of grass that separates the street and the parking lot.

"You think you and he are gonna start hanging out again?" Pete asked me.

"Well, he's probably done hanging around

with the wolves. And I don't think I'm going to spend much more time doing student council stuff," I said. "I'm not sure we have a choice. We might be stuck with each other."

"You could help him build his website."

"I am not going to help him make a website."

We reached the car and climbed inside. I took the passenger's seat, next to Dad.

"Are you guys okay?" Dad said, bags under his eyes. "What the heck happened in there? Your mother and I got a recording from the school on our answering machine. Kids injured? Jackie, holy geez, your neck—"

"We're all right," I said. "Just banged up. Last night—last night's going to take a lot of explaining."

"I'll let you tell it, Jack," Pete said, nestling in the back. He drifted to sleep almost instantly, lying down across both seats.

I looked back at him with a smile. He dragged his left arm over his face to block out sunlight from the car window.

Sleep tight, big brother, I thought. *You've earned it.*

I yawned, rubbed my eyes, and noticed a series of dots lining the side of Pete's hand. Dark red and raw-looking. Like bite marks.

Everything's fine in Bridgewater. Really . . .

Or is it?

Look for all the titles from the
Night Fall collection.

THE CLUB

Bored after school, Josh and his friends decide to try out an old board game. The group chuckles at Black Magic's promises of good fortune. But when their luck starts skyrocketing—and horror strikes their enemies—the game stops being funny. How can Josh stop what he's unleashed? Answers lie in an old diary—but ending the game may be deadlier than any curse.

THE COMBINATION

Dante only thinks about football. Miranda's worried about applying to college. Neither one wants to worry about a locker combination too. But they'll have to learn their combos fast—if they want to survive. Dante discovers that an insane architect designed St. Philomena High, and he's made the school into a doomsday machine. If too many kids miss their combinations, no one gets out alive.

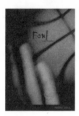

FOUL

Rhino is one of Bridgewater best basketball players—except when it comes to making free throws. It's not a big deal, until he begins receiving strange threats. If Rhino can't make his shots at the free throw line, someone will start hurting the people around him. Everyone's a suspect: a college recruiter, Rhino's jealous best friend, and the father Rhino never knew—who recently escaped from prison.

LAST DESSERTS

Ella loves to practice designs for the bakery she'll someday own. She's also one of the few people not to try the cookies and cakes made by a mysterious new baker. Soon the people who ate the baker's treats start acting oddly, and Ella wonders if the cookies are to blame. Can her baking skills help her save her best friend—and herself?

THE LATE BUS

Lamar takes the "late bus" home from school after practice each day. After the bus's beloved driver passes away, Lamar begins to see strange things—demonic figures, preparing to attack the bus. Soon he learns the demons are after Mr. Rumble, the freaky new bus driver. Can Lamar rescue his fellow passengers, or will Rumble's past come back to destroy them all?

LOCK-IN

The Fresh Start Lock-In was supposed to bring the students of Bridgewater closer together. Jackie didn't think it would work, but she didn't think she'd have to fight for her life, either. A group of outsider kids who like to play werewolf might not be playing anymore. Will Jackie and her brother escape Bridgewater High before morning? Or will a pack of crazed students take them down?

MESSAGES FROM BEYOND

Some guy named Ethan has been texting Cassie. He seems to know all about her—but she can't place him. Cassie thinks one of her friends is punking her. But she can't ignore how Ethan looks just like the guy in her nightmares. The search for Ethan draws her into a struggle for her life. Will Cassie be able to break free from her mysterious stalker?

THE PRANK

Pranks make Jordan nervous. But when a group of popular kids invite her along on a series of practical jokes, she doesn't turn them down. As the pranks begin to go horribly wrong, Jordan and her crush Charlie work to discover the cause of the accidents. Is the spirit of a prank victim who died twenty years earlier to blame? And can Jordan stop the final prank, or will the haunting continue?

THE PROTECTORS

Luke's life has never been "normal." His mother holds séances and his crazy stepfather works as Bridgewater's mortician. But living in a funeral home never bothered Luke—until his mom's accident. Then the bodies in the funeral home start delivering messages to him, and Luke is certain he's going nuts. When they start offering clues to his mother's death, he has no choice but to listen.

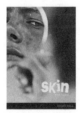

SKIN

It looks like a pizza exploded on Nick Barry's face. But a bad rash is the least of his problems. Something sinister is living underneath Nick's skin. Where did it come from? What does it want? With the help of a dead kid's diary, Nick slowly learns the answers. But there's still one question he must face: how do you destroy an evil that's inside you?

THAW

A storm caused a major power outage in Bridgewater. Now a project at the Institute for Cryogenic Experimentation is ruined, and the thawed-out bodies of twenty-seven federal inmates are missing. At first, Dani didn't think much of the news. Then her best friend Jake disappeared. To get him back, Dani must enter a dangerous alternate reality where a defrosted inmate is beginning to act like a god.

UNTHINKABLE

Omar Phillips is Bridgewater High's favorite local teen author. His Facebook fans can't wait for his next horror story. But lately Omar's imagination has turned against him. Horrifying visions of death and destruction come at him with wide-screen intensity. The only way to stop the visions is to write them down. Until they start coming true . . .

SOUTHSIDE HIGH

ARE YOU A SURVIVOR?

check out all the books in the

SURVIVING SOUTH SIDE

collection.

Bad Deal

Fish hates taking his ADHD meds. They help him concentrate, but they also make him feel weird. When a cute girl needs a boost to study for tests, Fish offers her a pill. Soon more kids want pills, and Fish likes the profits. To keep from running out, Fish finds a doctor who sells phony prescriptions. After the doctor is arrested, Fish decides to tell the truth. But will that cost him his friends?

Beaten

Paige is a cheerleader. Ty's a football star. They seem like the perfect couple. But when they have their first fight, Ty scares Paige with his anger. Then after losing a game, Ty goes ballistic and hits Paige. Ty is arrested for assault, but Paige still secretly meets up with him. What's worse—flinching every time your boyfriend gets angry, or being alone?

Benito Runs

Benito's father has been in Iraq for over a year. When he returns, Benito's family life is not the same. Dad suffers from PTSD—post-traumatic stress disorder—and yells constantly. Benito can't handle seeing his dad so crazy, so he decides to run away. Will Benny find a new life? Or will he learn how to deal with his dad—through good times and bad?

Plan B

Lucy has her life planned: she'll graduate high school and join her boyfriend at college in Austin. She'll become a Spanish teacher and of course they'll get married. So there's no reason to wait to sleep together, right? They try to be careful, but Lucy gets pregnant. Lucy's plan is gone. How will she make the most difficult decision of her life?

Recruited

Kadeem is Southside High's star quarterback. College scouts are seeking him out. One recruiter even introduces him to a college cheerleader and gives him money to have a good time. But then officials start to investigate illegal recruiting. Will Kadeem decide to help their investigation, though it means the end of the good times? What will it do to his chances of playing in college?

Shattered Star

Cassie is the best singer at Southside. She dreams of being famous. Cassie skips school to try out for a national talent competition. But her hopes sink when she sees the line. Then a talent agent shows up and tells Cassie she has "the look" he wants. Soon she is lying and missing glee club rehearsal to meet with him. And he's asking her for more each time. How far will Cassie go for her shot at fame?